THE IMAGINATION STATION

FOCUS ON THE FAMILY

Rescue on the River

BOOK 24

MARIANNE HERING AND SHEILA SEIFERT
ILLUSTRATIONS BY SERGIO CARIELLO

FOCUS
ON THE FAMILY.

A Focus on the Family Resource
Published by Tyndale House Publishers

This book is dedicated to Dani, a
woman of courage—MKH

To three amazing young women:
Jayme, Alyssa, and Lindsey—SS

Rescue on the River

© 2019 Focus on the Family. All rights reserved.

A Focus on the Family book published by Tyndale House Publishers, Carol Stream, Illinois 60188.

The Imagination Station, Adventures in Odyssey, and *Focus on the Family* and their accompanying logos and designs are federally registered trademarks of Focus on the Family, 8605 Explorer Drive, Colorado Springs, CO 80920.

TYNDALE and Tyndale's quill logo are registered trademarks of Tyndale House Ministries.

Cover design by Jim Cail and Michael Heath | Magnus Creative

Author photographs taken by Cary Bates/Focus on the Family, and used with permission. Illustrator photograph taken by Sergio Cariello, and used with permission.

For Library of Congress Cataloging-in-Publication Data for this title, visit http://www.loc.gov/help/contact-general.html.

For manufacturing information regarding this product, please call 1-855-277-9400.

For information about special discounts for bulk purchases, please contact Tyndale House Publishers at csresponse@tyndale.com, or call 1-855-277-9400.

Printed in the United States of America

ISBN 978-1-58997-993-2 HC
ISBN 978-1-64607-012-1 SC

27   26   25   24   23   22   21
7   6   5   4   3   2   1

Contents

Prologue

At the end of the last adventure, *Terror in the Tunnel*, Patrick and Beth met their friend Eugene outside a train station. He had been acting as an undercover spy. But he still looked younger than his real age because the Imagination Station had broken. He would continue to look like a teenager until the Station was fixed.

The adventurers helped protect Abraham Lincoln from assassins in Baltimore, Maryland. Beth and Patrick weren't sure Lincoln made it safely to Washington. Beth hoped he had. Patrick wanted to make sure Mr. Lincoln was sworn in as president.

Here's what happened outside that Baltimore train station.

● ● ●

The cousins and Eugene pushed through people to reach an alley across from the station. Behind them, voices in the crowd seemed to grow angrier and angrier.

Beth heard a train whistle. She turned toward Calvert Station. "I have to go back," she said. "I have to know if Mr. Lincoln is on that train!"

The glow of the Imagination Station appeared. Soon the Model T stood nearby.

"According to historical documents, Lincoln should have made it through to Washington, DC," Eugene said. "It's time to return to Whit's End. Are you ready?"

"No!" Patrick said. "We still have Mr. Lincoln's inauguration speech. He'll need it if he lives long enough to give it."

Beth lifted the oilskin bag. "May we go to Washington?" she asked Eugene. "We'll either see Mr. Lincoln give the speech, or we'll be there for his funeral."

"Very well," Eugene said.

This time Beth sat in the passenger seat. She held Lincoln's black bag tightly. Patrick sat in the rumble seat. Eugene sat behind the steering wheel.

He slammed his fist into the red button.

Blatt!

March 4, 1861

Beth opened her eyes. In front of her was a fancy hotel. The morning sun fought against gray clouds to light the hotel entrance.

Beth climbed out of the Imagination Station. She saw Patrick fumble with the seat belt in the rumble seat. He couldn't get out. Beth thought the Imagination Station was taking him to a different place.

Patrick waved to her as the Imagination Station faded.

Beth waved back until it disappeared. She trusted she would find him later. Then she entered the hotel.

Beth wandered through the crowd. She carefully sidestepped many men holding silk top hats. Several ladies also stood in the hotel lobby. They wore poufy dresses. Many had winter cloaks draped over their arms.

She saw Tad Lincoln dressed in a black suit. Tad was Abraham Lincoln's youngest son. Beth had met him on a previous adventure.

"Tad!" Beth shouted.

But Tad walked through a pair of French doors.

Beth followed him.

Willie Lincoln, another of Mr. Lincoln's sons, sat on the floor, playing with his toy metal soldiers. Beth thought Willie looked proper in his black bowtie.

Abraham Lincoln was sitting on a couch. He had a small writing desk balanced on his lap. Tad sat next to his father.

Beth sighed with relief. Lincoln had made it through Baltimore. She was glad to see for herself that the future president was okay.

Lincoln's eldest son, Robert, sat nearby in a high-backed chair. He was reading some papers. Beth guessed it was another draft of Lincoln's speech.

Beth slowly approached the couch. She raised the oilskin bag. "Ahem," she said.

The Lincolns looked up.

"You're back!" Tad said. He slid off the couch and hugged her.

"And you have the bag with Father's speech in it," Willie said. He stood.

Beth set the bag at Mr. Lincoln's feet.

Lincoln smiled at her. He opened the bag and took out his old speech. Then he said to Robert, "Read the speech you have."

Robert read:

It follows from these views that no state, upon its own mere motion, can lawfully get out of the Union; that resolves and ordinances to that effect are legally void; and that acts of violence within any state or states against the authority of the United States are insurrectionary.

Beth wished she knew what *ordinances* and *insurrectionary* meant. But she did know what Lincoln was saying. He believed that no state could leave the Union. But Beth knew seven states had already rebelled and formed the Confederate States of America. They were South Carolina, Mississippi, Alabama, Florida, Georgia, Louisiana, and Texas.

Robert read a few more lines.

Lincoln said, "Stop!"

Robert paused midsentence.

Lincoln smiled and said, "That's the phrase I was looking for!" He picked up a pen from the small desk on his lap. He scratched out words on the paper. Then he wrote down the new words.

Mary Lincoln entered the room. She moved directly to the window.

Beth walked toward her. Outside the window a great crowd of people filled the streets. Beth saw several men in military uniforms move through the crowds.

Beth curtsied to Mrs. Lincoln. "Good day."

Mary nodded. "I see you're dressed for the day's event."

Beth glanced down. She was wearing a green dress and a blue cloak. They were the ones she had worn the last time she had seen Mary.

In that adventure, Mrs. Lincoln had helped them free a slave named Sally at Niagara Falls.

"And you're also dressed for the inauguration," Beth said.

"Yes," Mrs. Lincoln said. Mary Lincoln smiled. The light from the crystal chandelier bounced off her shiny brown hair.

"You look beautiful," Beth said.

"Thank you," Mrs. Lincoln said. She glanced around the room. "Where's your cousin Patrick?"

"He's with a friend from home," Beth said.

"I'm glad your time at Niagara Falls was successful. I know because I have a message for you," Mrs. Lincoln said.

"A message?" Beth said.

Mrs. Lincoln nodded. She said, "I received a letter from Canada yesterday."

Beth's heart leaped with excitement. "Is it from Sally Culver?"

Mrs. Lincoln fished the letter out of her pocket. "It's from her employer, but the postscript is from Sally."

Beth started to read the note, but a loud voice broke into Beth's thoughts. She put the letter in her pocket. She would read it later.

"Mrs. Lincoln," said a man standing by the French doors. "It's time for you and the children to leave for the White House. Your carriage awaits."

The soon-to-be First Lady turned away from the window. "Come along, boys," she said to Willie and Tad. "This is going to be Mr. Lincoln's finest hour!"

Willie moved toward his mother. "May Beth come with us?" the boy asked.

"That's a splendid idea," Mr. Lincoln said. "Beth can help Mrs. Lincoln watch you boys."

"Yippee!" Tad shouted. He took Beth's hand and led her toward the door.

The Parade

Patrick climbed down from the rumble seat.

A still-young Eugene stepped out of the Imagination Station. He wore the same suit and top hat from the train station.

Patrick also wore the same brown suit he had been wearing earlier.

The two stood in a parklike area jam-packed with people. The machine faded.

Patrick didn't recognize anyone. He asked Eugene, "Where's Beth?"

Eugene said, "I sent her to the Willard Hotel. She's with the Lincolns."

"So he *is* alive?" Patrick asked.

"Observe," Eugene said.

Patrick looked around him. He saw a familiar white building with a dome on top. In front of the building were steps. They led up to a large flat area with a podium and grandstands.

Thousands of people in fancy clothes stood below the steps. Many held flags. More flags flew from nearby buildings.

Men in blue uniforms kept people from sitting in the grandstand seats. The men also kept the avenue in front of the building clear.

"That's the Capitol," Patrick said. He turned to Eugene in excitement. "Mr. Lincoln's alive! He's going to give his inaugural speech!"

Eugene nodded. "Indeed," he said. "I see

the militia is here to make sure it occurs as planned."

Suddenly Patrick felt a friendly slap on his back. He turned around.

Colonel Sumner stood before him. The military man's blue uniform was perfectly pressed. Its polished gold buttons shone. A dagger and a pistol hung from his belt.

Patrick had met Colonel Sumner on the previous adventure. The older, white-haired gentleman grinned a happy greeting.

"Mr. Lincoln is to arrive in less than twenty minutes," the colonel said.

Then the colonel turned aside. He spoke quietly to Eugene. Patrick heard the words *Mr. Pinkerton* and *killers*.

Eugene bowed to the colonel. He raised a hand in farewell to Patrick. "I have a certain mission to which I must attend," Eugene said.

"It's of a rather personal nature. You'll be all right here, I'm certain."

Patrick waved good-bye.

Eugene walked off.

Colonel Sumner pointed across the street toward the two- and three-story buildings. "Look there," he said to Patrick.

Patrick saw dozens of soldiers in loose blue jackets and brimmed caps. Each man held a rifle.

"Snipers!" Patrick said. "They must be there to protect Mr. Lincoln. How can I help?"

"I need you to sit behind the podium," Colonel Sumner said. "Make sure no one rushes Mr. Lincoln from behind."

Patrick gulped. *Would someone really shoot or stab Mr. Lincoln during his speech?* he wondered.

The colonel escorted Patrick through the line of military men. The soldiers saluted

Colonel Sumner. The colonel showed Patrick his place on the risers.

"I'll be off," Colonel Sumner said. "Thanks for your help, young man."

Patrick waved good-bye. The colonel left.

Just then a carriage pulled by four horses stopped. The carriage driver hopped down from his bench and opened the door.

Tad Lincoln jumped down. His brother Willie and his mother, Mary, followed him. Then a young girl climbed out.

"Beth, over here!" Patrick called. Patrick gave his cousin a wide and wild wave.

She waved back.

Soon they were all sitting in front of the Capitol. More carriages arrived, and important people sat near them. One of those men was Robert Lincoln.

Patrick looked up at the nearby rooftops. The snipers were in position.

A band started playing a patriotic tune.

"Imagine," Mrs. Lincoln said, "they're playing 'Hail to the Chief' for *my* husband!"

Patrick wondered if Mrs. Lincoln knew about the danger to her husband.

Several uniformed men on horses paraded down the avenue. They surrounded a small, open carriage.

Patrick stood on the top riser to get a better view. He looked out over the sea of people. Fine horses with tall feathers in their bridles pulled long floats.

Banners and flags decorated the floats. They represented states that had not left the Union.

A group of old soldiers proudly walked down the avenue.

"Those are the heroes of the War of 1812," Mary Lincoln said. "Let's hope our country never has to fight another war."

The Speech

The band began another song. A long line of men came out of the Capitol building. All were well dressed, and a few wore black robes. They took empty seats behind the canopy-covered podium.

Mrs. Lincoln whispered to the children. "Those men are congressmen, senators, and Supreme Court judges," she said. "And there's Mr. Buchanan, the former president."

Suddenly the crowd went wild.

The children stood on their chairs to watch.

Mr. Lincoln made a grand entrance as he walked out onto the podium. The crowd cheered.

Lincoln carried a gold-tipped cane. He had changed clothes since Beth had seen him that morning. His black suit and hat looked brand  new. He took off his hat and a man nearby offered to hold it.

Lincoln bowed low. The applause roared even louder.

Soon the people quieted.

Lincoln reached inside his jacket pocket and took out his speech. He spread the papers on the podium. He placed his cane on top to keep the papers from blowing away. Mr. Lincoln reached inside his pocket, pulled out spectacles and balanced them on his nose.

A man in the crowd below shouted, "Look at old four-eyes!"

Three policemen hurried to that spot. They escorted the loud-mouthed man away.

Lincoln began his speech in a strong voice. "Fellow citizens of the *United* States."

The crowd stopped his speech every few lines with cheers or claps.

Lincoln finished his speech by bowing his head as if in prayer.

Then an old judge with weathered skin and a hunched back moved forward. He wore a black robe. The judge's hand shook as he held out a Bible.

Lincoln put his hand on the Bible and said, "I, Abraham Lincoln, do solemnly swear that I will faithfully execute the office of president of the United States and defend the Constitution." Next, Lincoln took the Bible out

of the judge's hands. He kissed the holy book's well-worn cover.

Suddenly a blast of artillery fire filled the area.

Boom! Bang! Rat-a-tat-tat! Boom! Boom!

Beth's heart nearly beat out of her chest. *Is someone shooting at the president?*

● ● ●

Patrick ducked when he heard the gunfire. It echoed through the park. But then the crowd cheered almost as loud.

There was a pause as the cannon and rifles were reloaded.

"Mr. Lincoln!" Tad called.

"You mean Mr. President!" Willie shouted.

Abraham Lincoln turned and smiled at his sons. They ran to their father and hugged him.

Suddenly Patrick heard Eugene shout, "Beth! Patrick! Over here!"

Patrick scanned the crowd and spotted his friend.

Eugene waved his tall black hat at them. He headed toward them through the mob of people.

Just then two police officers came to escort Mrs. Lincoln to her carriage.

"Bless you both," Mary Lincoln said to the cousins. "Don't forget to read the postscript from Sally at the end of the letter." She left.

Patrick saw Beth pull a paper out of her cloak's pocket.

"Listen, Patrick," Beth said. She waved the letter.

But more artillery fire drowned her words.

"We've got to meet Eugene," Patrick said.

The cousins pushed past the crowds.

Eugene suddenly stepped out from behind a column.

"We have plenty of work ahead of us," Eugene

said. "I've been conferring with the militia leaders. They believe a civil war will start soon."

Beth sighed. "That means trouble for Sally's brother." She held the letter and read:

> *P.S. Dear Mrs. Lincoln, Please ask the honorable Mr. Lincoln to free the slaves in Beaufort, South Carolina. My brother Kitch was recently sent there. The conditions there are worse than in Kentucky.*

"Can we help Sally's brother?" Patrick asked.

"Hmm," Eugene said, "that will be difficult."

"Why?" Beth asked.

"South Carolina is in the Deep South," Eugene said. "And . . ."

"And what?" Patrick asked.

"Mr. Lincoln has not yet freed any of the slaves," Eugene said. "In his speech he said he's trying to save the Union first."

"But we have to do something!" Beth said.

Patrick heard a low humming noise. The Imagination Station appeared.

"I have to finish something here to get back to my proper age," Eugene said. "But you may go help Sally's brother. It will have to be after the war has started."

Patrick and Beth hurried toward the machine. Beth got in on the passenger side. Patrick sat in the driver's seat. He grabbed hold of the steering wheel.

The car seemed to surge forward. But everything Patrick saw through the windshield blurred. He saw only millions of dots of color.

Then the dots broke apart. They sprayed out of the machine like water droplets.

I'm driving through time again, Patrick thought.

And then suddenly, everything went black.

A Civil War Nurse

The Imagination Station landed. Patrick got out of the machine and closed the door. Beth stepped out of the passenger side.

They stood in a grove of trees with thick, gray bark. Patrick pushed a clump of leaves out of his way to see better. The trees around him were as tall as a five-story building. Their spring-green leaves spread across the blue sky.

The Imagination Station faded away.

The air was warm, but Patrick's feet felt cold and wet.

He looked down. Black water covered his brown shoes and red pants up to his ankles. His navy-blue jacket had gold buttons. He was now wearing a military uniform.

He had landed in a pond. Mosquitoes hovered over him. He checked his pocket and found a watch. The watch face had

a picture of a man sitting on a beautiful horse.

"Be careful," Beth said from behind him.

Patrick dropped the watch back into his pocket. He turned around to look at her.

Beth was wearing a red dress, boots, and a black coat. She was standing on leaf-covered high ground, a good distance away.

He swatted at a mosquito. "Be careful of what?" he asked.

Beth motioned toward one end of the pond.

Patrick looked where she was pointing. He saw more black water, large trees, and a log. The log moved, and Patrick took a double look. It was dark green and as long as a car.

An alligator!

Its mouth was clamped shut. But several of its sharp teeth jutted out. The beast's beady eyes glared at Patrick.

The alligator thrashed its tail. The motion propelled it through the water.

"Get out of there!" Beth shouted.

The beast moved toward Patrick. Its jaws opened wide enough to swallow Patrick's leg.

Patrick sprinted, his shoes sloshing in the shallow, muddy water.

He glanced over his shoulder.

The alligator neared the end of the pond and lunged. Its body rose out of the water.

Patrick took a huge step. He landed on the ground next to Beth.

The cousins scurried away from the water.

Patrick paused when he felt far enough away. He couldn't believe how big it was. He could see the alligator's cream-colored underside. The creature was half out of the water.

Then it quickly lunged again. Its cave-like jaws opened.

The cousins jumped backward. But the alligator's jaws clamped down on the edge of Beth's coat.

Beth shrieked.

The beast's head jerked to the right. Beth fell. Her arms flailed. The beast's tail and head thrashed.

Patrick quickly prayed to God for help. He

picked up a thick stick. He smashed it over the alligator's head.

Beth rolled out of her coat. She was free!

Patrick dropped the branch. He grabbed Beth's arm and pulled her up.

"Hurry!" he said.

They ran.

A cluster of trees was ahead of them.

"Climb that one," Patrick said, pointing to a thick tree.

Beth grabbed its low-hanging branch. She started to climb quickly.

Patrick grabbed the same branch. It was rough and scratchy. He pulled himself onto it after Beth reached the next tree limb.

They climbed until the branches were too thin for them go higher. They stopped and sat on a thick limb. They were completely hidden by leaves.

"Are we safe?" Beth asked, out of breath.

"Next time it might get my leg instead of just my coat."

Patrick tried to catch his breath. He glanced at the alligator below. He didn't want any more surprises.

The reptile's half-lidded eyes glared at the cousins. The beast walked back toward the pond, dragging Beth's coat with it. Then the creature slid into the water.

"My coat is ruined," Beth said. "And I'm not going near that water to get it. Good thing it's warm here."

"Now if we can just get rid of the mosquitoes," Patrick said. He swatted one.

● ● ●

Beth noticed clumps of hairlike strings hanging on the tree. She fingered the gray-green strands. They were soft and feathery.

"What is that?" Patrick asked.

"I think it's moss," Beth said.

Beth scanned the area. She saw a woman whose dark skin covered high cheekbones. Her brown hair was tied up in a colorful cloth. She wore a dress with long stripes. A leather bag hung from a strap on her shoulder.

The woman suddenly stopped and bent down. She dug up a plant with a knife she took from her bag. The roots were thick and brown.

The woman looked familiar.

She stepped closer to the pond. Beth's cloak was in the mud at the water's edge. The alligator was still there. It seemed to be waiting. It crept toward the woman.

"Look out!" Beth shouted to the woman.

The woman didn't seem to hear. She bent to dig up another root.

Patrick dropped to the ground. He picked up a branch. The alligator backed into the water.

"Be careful," Beth said. "That hungry creature is watching you."

The woman looked up. "I can take care of myself. These swamps are filled with healing plants," the woman said. "That's why I come."

Beth thought for a moment. The woman was a healer or a nurse. She was confident even though she dressed like a slave.

The woman added, "What business do you two have in a swamp with alligators?"

Patrick said, "I . . . we . . . I mean . . ."

Beth jumped down. She landed in the leaves next to Patrick. She finally recognized this woman. She said, "We've come to help you, Miss Tubman."

Patrick gasped. He said, "You're Harriet Tubman!"

Harriet Tubman

A slow smile spread across Harriet's lips. She gave a deep laugh. "You know me," Harriet said. "But I don't know you."

Beth said, "My name is Beth, and this is my cousin Patrick."

"You can call me Miss Harriet," she said. "Most people around here do."

"I've heard that you were also called Moses," Beth said.

"That was a name I used before the war," Harriet said. "When I was moving slaves along the Underground Railroad."

Harriet studied the cousins. "And there's plenty more slaves that need rescuing," she said. "Come along if you're going to help. Let's not give that alligator a dinner invitation." Harriet started walking.

Beth and Patrick had to half-run to keep up with her.

They reached a small stream and walked beside it. Dried leaves covered the banks. Tall trees gave them shade from the afternoon sun.

Beth noticed an envelope tucked in the pocket of her skirt. It was different from the letter with Sally's postscript. The Imagination Station must have given it as a gift. The cousins often received gifts when they went on adventures.

Beth pulled out the envelope. *John Adams,*

Colonel was written on it. The envelope was sealed.

Beth showed the letter to Patrick.

"The Imagination Station gave this to me," she said. "We may need to find someone named John Adams."

"Wasn't he a president?" Patrick asked.

Beth nodded. "But that was a long time ago," she said.

Beth tucked the note back in her pocket.

Patrick fished in his pants pocket. He took out the watch. He showed it to Beth.

"That's a Confederate officer on a warhorse," Beth whispered. "Someone wrote on the picture. It says Colonel William C. Heyward."

Patrick turned it over. *Follow the star* was inscribed on the back.

"Hide that watch," Beth said, "or Harriet might think we're Confederates. They're the enemy."

Soon the three of them left the shade of the trees. They came to a clearing filled with canvas tents.

"It's a tent city," Patrick said.

Some of the canvas tents looked like fabric houses. They had low walls and high, slanted roofs held up by poles and ropes. Other tents were cone-shaped like teepees.

Beth had never seen a city like this. She felt sweat drip down her forehead. It had been warm in the shade of the trees. It was much hotter among the tents in the late afternoon.

Harriet stopped in front of a tent. It was wider and longer than the others. The flaps were open. Inside were rows of narrow cots. Each one held a resting man.

Beth asked, "How did these men get sick?"

Harriet set her leather bag on the ground near a fire pit. "More soldiers die of diseases than in battle," she said.

Harriet started a fire in the pit. Then she picked up two tin coffeepots by their arched handles. She handed one each to Beth and Patrick.

The coffeepots were large. But they weren't too heavy.

"Fill these at the creek," Harriet said. "I'll get someone to show you where the cleanest water is." She moved to a group of black men in uniform. They were sitting in front of a tent. One walked back with her.

"This is Walter," Harriet said. She threw a big log on the fire.

Walter was a young teen in full uniform. He had a newspaper tucked underneath his arm. "What're you *white* children doing here?" he asked. He seemed curious, not angry.

"We came to help free the slaves," Beth said.

"Well, I never," said the lad. "Welcome to the Second South Carolina Volunteers."

"Thank you," Patrick said. "My name is Patrick, and this is my cousin Beth."

Beth studied their new friend. He looked handsome in the navy-blue jacket and red pants. His uniform was similar to Patrick's. But Walter's had army stripes on it. "You seem young to be a soldier," she said.

"I'm a drummer and run errands," he said. "I also speak Gullah. That's the language the plantation slaves speak."

Walter picked up an empty coffeepot and pointed. "The creek's this way," he said. The three of them started walking.

Beth glanced at the newspaper. The date on it was May 24, 1863. "Is that a current newspaper?" she asked.

"Current for us," Walter said. "It's only a week old. Miss Harriet gets people to teach us our letters. I read whenever I can."

"Me too," Beth said. She figured it had been just over two years since President Lincoln's inauguration.

Patrick asked, "How did your unit get so deep in enemy territory?"

Walter laughed. His smile showed his broad white teeth.

"We didn't *get* here," he said. "We are *from*

here—escaped slaves mostly. Except for about 130 men who came from Florida."

Patrick kicked a rock in his path. "What does your regiment do?" he asked.

"We raid plantations," Walter said. "That's how we get some of our food. We also have orders to free slaves. The colonel wants to weaken the enemy and get their slaves to fight against them."

"But right now we need to fill these coffeepots," Beth said.

She noticed a few logs floating in the water. They moved with the flow of the creek.

"Are those alligators?" she asked Walter.

He shook his head. "They look like regular logs, but be careful," he said. "The Confederates have hidden torpedoes along the shore."

Beth gulped. *Torpedoes?*

The Spy

The three walked back to camp with their coffeepots full of water. Walter set his coffeepot on Harriet's fire.

Patrick set his coffeepot on the fire too. Beth set hers next to the fire pit.

"Thank you," Harriet said. She gave them a smile. It brightened her weatherworn face.

Harriet used some water to clean the roots in her bag. Then she pulled out her knife and chopped them. She dropped the roots into both pots on the fire.

"We're looking for a slave named Kitch," Patrick said.

Walter said, "I haven't heard that name around these parts."

"He's a slave from Kentucky. He came a couple of years ago," Beth said. "And we're also looking for John Adams." She fingered the letter in her pocket.

"I don't know anyone named Kitch," Harriet said. "But you'll need to go to the river for John Adams."

Steam was soon pouring out of the coffeepot spouts. The concoction smelled like a spiced tea.

Harriet turned to Walter. "Take that pot to the big hospital tent," she said. "Tell the nurses it's for the contraband with stomach problems. The men will be healed in no time."

Beth wondered what *contraband* meant. But she didn't interrupt.

"Glad to help," Walter said. He used the newspaper to pick up the pot by the hot handle. He moved away with the medicine.

Harriet turned and started walking between tents.

Beth and Patrick hurried after her.

"Miss Harriet," Beth said, "what is contraband?"

"Freed slaves," she said. "Slaves escape their plantations. They come to Union camps for protection. Many think of them as spoils of war or property."

"But slaves are people, not property," Patrick said.

"I wish everyone thought like that," Harriet said. "Then I wouldn't have to dress like a slave and sneak around as a spy."

"You're a spy?" Beth said.

Harriet laughed and winked. She said, "I'm fifty years old. How can I be a spy?"

"No one would suspect you," Patrick said.

Harriet gave him a smile and a wink. "That's right. People in the Deep South think slaves are stupid. So they talk freely around black people. Sometimes they even reveal their secrets."

"People do that to children, too," Beth said.

Harriet nodded. "I'm a nurse and a spy and whatever the good Lord wants me to be. It's all to help free slaves."

Harriet stopped where two paths crossed. "I must leave you here," she said. Then she pointed to her left. "That path takes you to the river. You'll find what you're looking for. Wait there for Walter."

Harriet took the path to her right and kept walking.

"Race you to the river," Beth said. She didn't wait for Patrick's reply. She took off running.

"No fair!" Patrick said.

They both ran hard.

The cousins reached the river together. The water was dark and murky, almost black.

Beth put a hand to her nose. The place had a sour odor. It was as if someone had just lit one hundred matches.

"What is that sulfur smell?" Beth asked. "Are there rotten eggs around here?"

Patrick looked at the wide river in front of them. There were three ships on the water. Several rowboats were moving between the ships and the shore.

"I can't tell you about the smell," Patrick said. "But I found *John Adams*."

The John Adams

Patrick pointed toward a ship with *John Adams* written on its side. It looked like a ferryboat with two large paddlewheels. The ship's hull didn't reach very high above the water. But it had a large deck.

Two empty masts stuck up like straws in a milkshake. Two large, black smokestacks rose out of the center of the deck. The stars and stripes of the Union flag flew at the ship's bow.

"Maybe I need to give my letter to someone on that ship," Beth said.

"I think you're right," Patrick said. He studied the second ship, the *Harriet A. Weed*. It was similar to the *John Adams*. But the deck was even larger.

Beth pointed to a ship named the *Sentinel*. "That one has a taller hull," she said.

Walter approached the cousins.

"Hi, Walter," Patrick said.

"Why does it smell like rotten eggs around here?" Beth asked the drummer.

Walter laughed. "The smell comes from the mud along the river. It's called pluff mud," Walter said. "Some love it, and some hate it. To me it just smells like home."

Patrick hoped he would soon get used to the odor. But he had his doubts.

"Those ships are beauties," Walter said, pointing toward them. "The *John Adams* has a lot of big guns. The *Harriet A. Weed* has two cannons. The *Sentinel* doesn't have any artillery. But it's still a good ship."

Walter turned toward Patrick. "Would you help me row some boxes out to the *Adams*?"

"Not without me," Beth said. "I'm coming too."

Walter laughed. "You're just like Miss Harriet," he said. "She doesn't keep from hard work either."

They spent several hours using rowboats to move boxes to each ship. The boxes had food and medical supplies in them.

Patrick scooted his last box on the deck of the *Sentinel*. It made a shushing sound like sandpaper on wood.

He was tired. The evening had slipped into darkness. Hundreds of stars shone in the night sky.

More soldiers from Walter's unit climbed aboard the *Sentinel*. Groups of white soldiers also climbed aboard. They huddled together in small groups on the deck. The embers from pipes and cigars cast a reddish glow on their faces.

"That's the last of the supplies," Walter said. On top of the crate was a drum. It had a black shoulder strap attached to it.

Beth joined them. Her shoulders drooped, and she looked tired.

"I see we have new recruits," Harriet said from behind him.

Beth smiled. "When did you get here?" she asked.

"I just made it on," Harriet said. "I wouldn't miss it." Patrick felt the ship move as the engines came on. The large wheel churned against the water. "Miss what?" he asked.

Harriet said, "Tonight we're going on a raid. We're going to bring as many slaves as we can to freedom."

Waiting for Trouble

Beth worried about what might happen on a raid. Her stomach felt knotted. She listened to the slow chugging of the *Sentinel*. The sound comforted her.

Beth strained to see ahead. But the river was covered with darkness.

Walter held a lantern. Its glow was barely stronger than a jack-o'-lantern's.

"The stars are nice," Beth said. "But I wish there was a moon out tonight."

"Thank the Lord there isn't," Harriet said. "We waited for a night like this. We don't want anyone to see us."

"How will the captain know where we're going?" Beth asked.

Walter laughed. He said, "The pilots are guiding these ships, not the white captains. They have traveled these rivers for years. They know where the torpedoes are hidden."

"Torpedoes?" Patrick asked. His eyes grew large.

"I doubt there are any on this river. But if there are," Walter said, "our pilots will know about them."

"We won't reach our first stop until dawn," Harriet said. "That's on the Combahee River. It's about twenty-five miles from here."

Walter added, "Our targets are the rice plantations along the Combahee."

"Rice?" Patrick asked.

"Of course," Walter said. "In these parts it's known as Carolina Gold."

"What do you do on a raid?" Beth asked.

"Whatever we can to help the Union soldiers," Harriet said. "My goal is to free as many slaves as I can."

"We'll take whatever supplies we can," Walter said. "Then we'll destroy everything else."

"If all goes well," Harriet said, "we'll be back here by tomorrow night."

But what if all doesn't go well? Beth wondered. The Confederates could attack. A ship could sink. She and Patrick could be taken as prisoners along with their new friends. People could even be killed.

Beth heard something sliding into the water. She remembered the alligator. Above them a bird gave a shrill *ca-ca-ca*.

She heard a slight hum and looked into the

darkness. The Imagination Station appeared. But it was fading in and out. The young Eugene was driving it.

The Model T was headed toward them. It was going fast. Beth ducked.

"Are you okay?" Patrick asked.

Beth looked around. The Imagination Station had disappeared. She said, "Did you see that?"

"See what?" Patrick asked.

Thud!

They all lurched forward. Beth fell onto the deck on her hands and knees.

Patrick landed next to her.

"What did we crash into?" Patrick asked.

A whirring sound came from the ship's engine. But the vessel didn't move.

"Let's find out what happened," Walter said.

They moved toward a crowd gathered around a man. He wore light-colored clothes, not a uniform. Beth guessed he was a pilot.

A soldier asked, "Why aren't we moving?"

The captain hurried to the front of the crowd. "The mission is still on," he said. "But the *Sentinel* has run aground. Fortunately, the other ships can travel in shallower water."

Harriet sighed and said, "Our part of this mission is over. Godspeed to the other boats."

Beth listened for the other ships. But she didn't hear any chugging.

"The *Adams* and *Weed* are probably miles away," Harriet said. "Let's pray that many slaves will be freed."

Patrick and Beth held hands. Harriet said, "Lord, we're going to hold steady on You. And You've got to see us through."

Patrick said, "Amen."

"It might be a long wait," Walter said. He lay down on the deck. "I'm going to get some sleep."

Beth stayed alert. Now nothing felt safe.

"I don't like waiting," Harriet said. "But sometimes waiting is all we can do."

"How much danger are we in?" Beth asked.

"We should be okay," Walter said from where he lay on the deck. "The Union controls this area."

"It does," Harriet said. "But Confederates sneak into Union-controlled areas. And we sneak into their territory."

Beth thought she heard something. She wasn't sure what it was at first.

She heard Walter start to snore and a bird trill. There was a muffled splash of water. But then she heard it again. It was a repeated rhythm, something between a rumble and a hiss.

And the sound slowly drew closer. It became a soft chugging noise.

Harriet said, "That sounds like a steam engine."

"Any steamship out at this time of night is up to no good," Patrick said.

"Sneaking, just like we are," Beth said.

Everyone on deck grew quiet.

"It's dark," Harriet said in a low voice. "Maybe they won't see us. Stay low to keep away from flying bullets. Behind a crate is safest."

Walter continued snoring.

The soldiers put out their lanterns. They rested their rifles on the ship's railing. Beth knew they were getting ready for an attack.

Beth put out Walter's lamp.

Harriet moved between Patrick and Beth. She grabbed their hands and pulled them behind a crate.

"Hide here," she said. She went back for Walter.

Beth started to shiver. She didn't like the idea of being in a real Civil War battle.

Banished

The chugging came closer and closer.

Beth and Patrick held hands. There was nothing they could do but wait.

Quietly, Walter and Harriet joined the cousins. They all hid behind the crate.

Patrick heard the hum of the Imagination Station. He peeked over the crate.

An older Eugene was in the Model-T car. He was driving toward Patrick. But he was only a shimmer. Then he was gone.

"Did you see Eugene?" Patrick whispered.

Beth shook her head. "I thought I saw him earlier. Something must have gone wrong."

Patrick saw a long shadow move beside their ship. The other ship's lanterns were lit. A man stood on the edge of the boat. He held his lantern high.

Maybe he won't see us, Patrick thought.

The chugging stopped. The boat slowed.

"Ahoy there," said a deep voice on the other ship. "Need some help?"

The captain called out, "We've run aground."

The voice from the other ship said, "We'll take you aboard."

Harriet peeked over the crate. "I recognize that voice," she said. "That's James Montgomery. He's aboard the *Adams*."

"We're saved!" Beth said.

"And Miss Harriet will get to go on the raid," Patrick said.

Montgomery called, "Start rowing the cargo over and then your soldiers. We'll leave the *Sentinel* behind."

Patrick heard another chugging sound.

Walter squinted into the night. He said, "That's the *Weed*. They both came back for us."

Walter hurried to help the soldiers. Some pushed wooden crates to the edge. Others untied the rowboats behind the ship.

Patrick tried pushing a heavy crate. It wouldn't budge.

Beth helped Patrick push. Slowly they moved the crate to the edge of the boat. The *Adams* was only a stone's throw away. Cargo and people were being ferried over quickly.

"It's a delay," Harriet said. "But we can still raid the rice plantations."

The cousins waited for their turn in a rowboat. Harriet and Walter boarded first. Soon it was Beth's turn. She climbed down the rope ladder.

Then it was Patrick's turn. He jumped and landed. His shoes made a thud against the wooden rowboat. He sat next to Beth.

Then three soldiers quickly boarded. One of them picked up the back pair of oars.

The rowboat sunk deeper in the water. Patrick heard something bump against its side. He wondered if alligators came to the middle of rivers.

"Enough," a soldier said. "These boats only hold eight passengers. We already have more than that."

The soldiers dipped their oars into the water. It took only a few strokes to reach the *Adams*. The soldiers climbed out. Walter and Miss Harriet did too.

Beth made her way up the rope ladder and onto the ship.

"Thank you for rowing us," Patrick said. He started to climb the rope ladder. His feet left the boat.

The soldier started rowing away.

Patrick took a deep breath and finished his climb. Finally he was at the ship's edge. He felt Walter pulling him onto the ship.

"Thanks," he said to Walter.

Suddenly a man shouted, "Not on my ship!" It was James Montgomery's voice.

The man held a lantern. The glow lit up his face. Montgomery had dark curly hair and wore a bushy beard and moustache.

He looked at Beth, then at Patrick.

Montgomery shook his head. The lantern swayed back and forth. The shifting light made him look scary.

"Neither of you can be here," Montgomery said. "You're children. There's no place in battle for children."

"They're with me, Colonel Montgomery," Harriet said.

Colonel! Patrick exchanged glances with Beth.

Montgomery's face softened. "Not even for you, Miss Harriet," the colonel said. "Remove the children from this ship."

Suddenly Beth spoke. "Colonel," she said, "I have a letter for you." She took the envelope from her pocket. She held out the letter to him.

Montgomery took it from her. He gave the lantern to a soldier beside him.

"Hold the lantern high," he said.

He opened the envelope.

Patrick held his breath.

The colonel read the letter under the lantern. He grunted.

"I don't like this at all," the colonel said. He pointed at Beth. "You can stay."

She smiled.

Patrick let out his breath. The letter had saved them.

The colonel turned and pointed to Patrick. "But *not* you," he said.

"What?" Beth said. "We have to stay together."

"No," the man said. "The note is from Major General Sumner. He vouches for the bearer of the note. He says nothing about the bearer's companions."

Beth turned to Patrick. Her eyes were big with worry.

The colonel turned to the soldier holding the lantern. He said, "Get that boy off my ship."

The Harriet A. Weed

"No!" Beth said. "That's not fair!"

"You're welcome to join him, young lady," Montgomery said. "Get this boy off the *Adams* now."

A soldier came to Patrick's side. Patrick's shoulders drooped. He walked with the soldier to the edge of the ship. The rowboat was back, filled with crates from the *Sentinel*. Soldiers quickly unloaded it.

"Take that rowboat," the colonel said to Patrick.

Harriet hugged Patrick. "I'm sorry to see you go," she said. "But be sure the good Lord has another plan for you."

"Thank you, Miss Harriet," Patrick said.

Beth reached out and touched Patrick's arm.

"It's okay, Beth," Patrick said. "I'll be fine. You're going on the raid. Be safe."

"Time to go," said the soldier.

Patrick climbed down the rope ladder. Walter followed him. Beth hurried to the side of the ship to watch Patrick leave.

"I'll row," Walter said to the rower.

"Thanks," said the soldier. He climbed out of the rowboat.

Beth saw Walter sit in the boat. He took the oars in his hands. Patrick sat in the middle of the boat. The rowboat moved away from the ship.

Beth waved to Patrick.

Patrick waved back. He tried to look cheerful, but Beth could tell he was sad.

Harriet slipped a comforting arm around Beth. "Come away, child."

Beth nodded. She wiped a tear from her eye. She would go on this raid. She would do whatever she could to help Harriet free others.

"We have a long way to go," Harriet said to Beth. "And we need to be awake when we get there. Let's get some sleep."

Harriet walked between some crates. There was room for two people to lie down. Harriet lay down and turned on her side. She used the crook of her arm as a pillow.

Beth followed her lead. But she doubted she would be able to sleep. She looked up into the night sky.

Suddenly she heard a low hum. Once again the Imagination Station appeared. But she saw only the front half of it. Young Eugene drove it. Then old Eugene was driving it. Then young Eugene drove it again.

The Model T disappeared.

Maybe Eugene was in more trouble than Patrick!

Patrick sat in the back of the rowboat. He said, "Would you sneak me back to the ship? I can hide inside a crate."

"No," Walter said. "I'm a soldier, Patrick. I have to obey my officers."

"I understand," Patrick said. He sighed.

"Being a soldier is about trusting your leaders," Walter said. "I can't disobey Colonel Montgomery's orders. I'd be cut from the regiment or get myself killed."

Patrick sighed again. He picked up the oars and rowed steadily.

"Cheer up," Walter said. He dipped his oars back into the water.

The *Sentinel* was only a few strokes away. The cold air brushed past them.

Walter passed the stranded boat.

"What're you doing?" Patrick asked.

"I have to obey my orders," Walter said. He smiled. "The colonel told me to take you off the *Adams*. But he didn't tell me exactly where to take you, did he?"

Patrick smiled.

"There's no one on the *Sentinel*," Walter

said. "I can't leave you alone there. I have to take you to the *Weed*."

"Thank you!" Patrick said quietly.

"I'm only doing my job," Walter said.

Both boys climbed on board the *Weed* and secured the rowboat.

"You're a little young to be on a raid," said a man's voice.

Not again! Patrick thought.

Patrick looked at the man. He was dressed like the pilot of the ship.

"We all have to do our part, sir," Patrick said.

"Colonel Montgomery asked that I take him off the *Adams*," Walter said. "This is the only other working boat, Simmons."

Simmons smiled.

"Sir, do you know of a slave named Kitch?" Patrick asked. "He's from Kentucky."

Simmons shrugged. "Hundreds of slaves

were moved to the Deep South since the war started," he said. "I don't know their names. They're spread out all over Beaufort County."

Patrick thought about asking the pilot about the picture on his watch. What did the inscription *Follow the star* mean? But he was afraid Simmons would think he was a Rebel— a Confederate soldier.

Simmons gave a nod and went on his way.

"He's a great pilot," Walter said. "We'll reach the Combahee River without hitting any buried torpedoes or running aground."

Patrick said, "What do we do now?"

"Rest," Walter said. "The raiding will start at dawn."

Patrick found a spot near the wheelhouse and sat down. Walter sat next to him.

"Besides, my nap was cut short," Walter said. Patrick could hear the smile in his voice.

"What do you expect to happen tomorrow?" Patrick asked.

"Hard to tell," Walter said. "First we have to clear the area of sniper fire. We don't want artillery shooting at us from the bluffs near the river. Then our boats can raid the plantations and free the slaves."

"What happens to those who are clearing the bluffs?" Patrick asked. "Will they go home another way?"

"The ships will pick them up on the way back down the river," Walter said. "Best not to think about it. Some of us will make it home to Beaufort, and some won't."

Patrick gulped. How could he fall asleep now?

11

Fields Point

Beth woke to the sound of soldiers' heavy footsteps. They thumped the deck of the *Adams*. She sat up and glanced around.

Harriet was no longer next to her.

The *Adams* had docked on the edge of the river. A small company of men was starting to leave the ship.

The dawn glowed bright orange on the horizon downriver. A large bluff rose ahead.

It looked like a mountain that someone had flattened at the top. Lush trees grew on its side.

Beth stood, and Harriet came toward her. "The land around the Combahee is beautiful, isn't it?" Harriet said. "This is Fields Point."

"Are we going to free the slaves now?" Beth asked.

"Not yet," Harriet said. "Fields Point has Confederate trenches dug on the top. Enemy snipers could be hiding there. The soldiers must clear the point if riverboats are to be safe. Let's stay behind the cannon."

Beth hurried behind the cannon with Harriet. She looked toward the bluff. The enemy might be preparing to shoot at them right now.

A dozen soldiers were climbing the side of the bluff.

Beth worried for them. Men in the trenches above could easily shoot them.

"Those soldiers and their captain are brave," Harriet said. She gently pulled Beth back farther behind the cannon. "Stay low."

Beth ducked and waited to hear the first shot.

● ● ●

Patrick stood on the deck of the *Weed*. He watched the soldiers leave the *Adams*. They wound their way through the trees toward Fields Point.

Walter nudged Patrick. "Get ready to salute," Walter said. "Here comes the major."

Patrick noticed the extra decorations on the shoulders of the man's uniform. Patrick raised his right hand in a salute to the major.

"Walter," said the major, "you and the other drummer catch up with the men."

Patrick realized he was "the other drummer."

"Yes, sir, Major," Walter said. "Then what?"

The major frowned. "Watch what happens there, of course," he said. "Then come back and give a report."

Patrick gulped. They would have to cross the river to follow the men. The ships' cannons couldn't protect an open rowboat.

The major added, "Take cover in the marshes by the shore if you hear shots."

"Yes, sir," Walter said. He saluted the major.

Patrick did the same.

Walter smiled at Patrick. "We're going to get in on some of the fun."

The boys quickly climbed into a rowboat and rowed to shore. The river was calm. Patrick listened for gunfire. He only heard the *ca-ca-ca* of birds and an occasional *bloop* of a fish in the water.

Patrick and Walter got out of the rowboat. They pulled it onto the shore. Slowly they climbed to follow the other Union soldiers.

The climb was hard at first. Large trees blocked them. Their branches pricked Patrick's skin. The rotten-egg smell filled Patrick's nostrils.

Patrick listened closely. He could barely hear the other Union men climbing. He finally reached the edge of the bluff behind Walter.

Slowly they sneaked toward the trenches. But he was surprised. No one was fighting.

Patrick peeked around a large tree. The Union soldiers stood at the top of the cliff. From the lookout point, the river could be seen for miles each way.

The captain of the group picked up a gray blanket off the ground. "It's still warm," he said. "The enemy was just here."

Patrick was glad the captain's men had taken the bluff without a shot. He hurried to Walter's side.

"Captain," Walter said, saluting the man. "We're here to bring word to the ships."

"Good," the captain said.

One of the soldiers pointed toward open land. "What's that?" he asked.

Patrick squinted to see in the distance. Confederates were retreating. One, two, three, four . . . Patrick saw five men riding away.

The captain motioned for half his men to follow them. The other soldiers guarded the bluff.

"Tell Colonel Montgomery what you saw. He needs to know," the captain said to Walter. "Some of us are going after the Confederates on foot. We don't want them sending for help. If they bring artillery to the lookout points, the enemy will sink our ships."

"Yes, sir," Walter said.

The captain pointed at Patrick. "You come

with us. You can take a message by foot to Tar Bluff once we know where the Rebels are."

"Yes, sir," Patrick said.

Patrick looked at Walter. Walter gave him a nod and a smile. Then Patrick hurried after the captain.

Beth stood on the deck of the *Adams*. She placed a ladle across a barrel full of sweet, clean water. She had just helped Harriet fill the soldiers' canteens.

A company of soldiers was leaving in rowboats. Their mission was to take control of the area at Tar Bluff. If they weren't successful, enemy soldiers could stop the mission. The Volunteers wouldn't be able to free the slaves.

"Can I get a refill?" a familiar voice asked Beth. Walter held out his plate-sized canteen.

Beth was surprised to see Walter on the *Adams*. She picked up the ladle and dipped it in the water. She filled Walter's round canteen.

Harriet and others moved closer to Walter. "Did you just talk with Colonel Montgomery? What happened on Fields Point?" Harriet asked.

"The Confederate soldiers fell back," Walter said. "The captain has secured Fields Point

and has left several men there. He's chasing
the Confederates on foot. He doesn't want
them warning the other Rebels. He's taken a
messenger with him to send word."

"Good," Harriet said.

Beth saw a gleam of hope in her eyes.

"I hope we seize Fields Point
and Tar Bluff," Harriet said.
"If we do, the raid will go
even better than planned.
And no shots have been
fired. That's a miracle."

The *Adams* started
to move back into the
center of the river. The
Weed followed.

"Are we going to
leave the soldiers
behind?" Beth
asked.

"We'll be back for them," Harriet said. She left with a wave and headed toward the colonel.

"When will we come back for them?" Beth asked.

"We'll come back this way on our way home," Walter said. He turned to Beth and shook his head. "I didn't mean for this to happen."

"For what to happen?" Beth asked.

"I took Patrick to the *Weed*, not the *Sentinel*," he said.

Beth smiled. "But that's good news," she said.

"It would be," Walter said. "But we were both sent as messengers to Fields Point. Patrick is still out there. He's all alone, and he's headed to Tar Bluff. That area is behind enemy lines."

The Chase

The captain crept toward a thick bush near a grove of trees. Patrick followed. They were not far from Fields Point. The captain raised a finger to his lips and whispered, "Shhh."

Patrick nodded. He and the captain were spying on the Confederate leader and his messenger. The other Union soldiers kept following the retreating Confederates.

Patrick peeked between the bright-green leaves.

The Confederate officer was talking to a young soldier. Their two horses were several feet away. The boy looked close to Patrick's age. He wore a gray uniform. The boy's flat-topped hat tilted forward on his head.

The officer said something to the boy. Patrick leaned forward to listen. But he couldn't hear what they were saying.

The boy hurried to the horse. He put a foot into the stirrup and mounted the horse.

The Confederate officer swatted the horse's backside. The animal took off at a run.

The captain rushed toward the Confederate officer. The man disappeared into the grove of trees.

Only the officer's horse remained. Patrick grabbed its reins to keep it from running away.

The captain yelled at Patrick, "Go after the messenger!"

He tossed Patrick a map. "Forget about Tar Bluff. Don't let that boy reach the Confederate base. He will warn the enemy, and our raid will be spoiled. The lives of all those on our ships may depend on you."

Patrick stuffed the map in his jacket pocket. He put a foot in the stirrup and swung his leg over the saddle.

The captain started after the officer again. But then he turned. "If you don't catch him, warn the colonel," he said. Then he disappeared into the trees.

Patrick grabbed the reins in one hand. With the other, he clenched a fistful of the horse's mane.

Patrick dug his heels into the horse's

flanks. "Giddyap!" he shouted. Then he slapped the reins across the horse's neck.

The horse bolted into the shadow of the trees.

Patrick could see the Confederate messenger in the distance. He was riding at a gallop.

Patrick slapped the reins again. "Hiyaa!" he shouted.

They raced through the trees. Patrick's horse dodged tree trunks and thick roots. He gripped the saddle with his knees to stay on.

Suddenly the sunlight shone brighter. He'd reached a dirt road.

The Confederate messenger's horse sprinted farther ahead on the dirt-packed path.

Patrick leaned forward in the saddle. "Come on, girl," he whispered in the horse's ear. "You can do better than this. People are depending on us!"

● ● ●

Beth watched as the soldiers quietly climbed Tar Bluff. They made it to the trenches on top.

Harriet stood by Beth and Walter.

"There's only one road that goes to the plantations from here. Enemy soldiers at Tar Bluff can stop ships on the river. They can stop people on the road with cannon fire or guns," Harriet said. "I hope we can take control of Tar Bluff. If we don't, we won't be able to help free any slaves."

The three waited and watched. Silence. Once again, no shots were fired. Perhaps there wouldn't be any fighting at all on this raid.

At least that's what Beth hoped.

Beth scoured the landscape. She looked up and down the bluff. She scanned the shoreline. There was no sign of Patrick, no sign of the enemy.

Finally Beth saw a Volunteer on top of the bluff. But he disappeared over the ridge.

Montgomery started shouting orders from across the deck. The *Adams* was on the move again.

Beth hurried to Walter's side. She said, "Shouldn't Patrick have been at Tar Bluff by

now? Or did you mean we'd pick him up here on our way home?"

Walter was silent for a moment. Then he said, "By foot it's only a mile. Patrick had plenty of time to get here. Unless he met the enemy."

The Cannons

Patrick felt as if he'd been riding for an hour. The Confederate messenger was getting farther ahead. Patrick didn't know how to make his horse go faster.

Streams of smoke filled the sky to the east. He heard the echo of rifle shots from the same direction. A battle was going on near the river.

The land between Patrick and the river looked like a shallow pond. Orderly rows of green plants grew in the water. Nearer to Patrick, an enormous garden covered the land.

Is this a plantation with a rice field? Patrick wondered. He could see slaves of all ages wading in the pond. They were bent over in ankle-deep water. There were trenches between the rows of plants for water to go through.

The men were shirtless. Their backs glistened with sweat. The women wore light-colored fabric draped around their bodies and heads. Their dresses were pulled above their knees so the fabric wouldn't get wet.

Children followed the women. Babies clung to their mothers' backs or were carried by older children.

No one seemed to notice Patrick.

He urged his horse on. It followed the messenger to the west, down a wide, graveled

road. Patrick saw a sign that said Stocks
Road. He pulled back the reins.

"Whoa," he said.

A flag was flying from the top of a large
building. But it wasn't the Union flag.

Patrick had seen this flag before in books.
It had a red background with a blue X from
corner to corner. It was the Confederate flag.

He was riding straight toward the enemy
headquarters.

● ● ●

Beth watched the *Weed* drop off soldiers to
raid a plantation. That ship was going to
remain there to support those troops.

The *Adams* continued to the Heyward
plantation. The deck held a mix of Volunteers
and white soldiers.

Beth and Harriet stood next to a covered
barrel. They were using it as a table. They

helped soldiers fill paper cartridges of ammunition with gunpowder.

Beth nodded toward the white soldiers. "Are they a part of the Volunteers?" she asked.

"No," Harriet said. "They are the Third Rhode Island Heavy Artillery regiment. They are trained to fire the cannons."

Beth carefully poured gunpowder onto a small piece of paper. Then she rolled it. Harriet twisted the ends to seal the gunpowder inside. Then Harriet carefully handed the cartridge to a soldier.

Walter paced the deck. He was practicing his drumming. His sticks made a *rat-a-tat-tat* on his round drum.

Suddenly there was a *bang*. Then another. The sound was coming from a distance.

"That's rifle fire," Harriet said. "Lord, have mercy. The Union boys are being fired at."

"More likely our men are firing at the slave

owners, Miss Harriet," Walter said. "Those South Carolina Volunteers are tough soldiers."

Beth could see smoke billowing on the horizon. "What's burning?" she asked.

"Everything," Harriet said. "The orders were to take everything the men can carry. Then they are to burn the rice stores, as well as food, barns, bridges, and houses. But Union soldiers are leaving the slave houses alone."

"Why?" Beth asked. "All the slaves will be free."

Harriet put a hand on Beth's head. "I wish that were so, child," she said. "But the ships have room to take only six or seven hundred people. The *Sentinel* was to take more, but it ran aground."

Walter added, "Many will be left behind. The Heyward plantation alone has several hundred slaves."

Several hundred? Beth thought. Her hopes

sank. How would she and Patrick find Kitch?
She was stuck on the ship, and Patrick was
missing.

She quickly bowed her head and prayed,
Please, God, help us find Sally's brother.
It seems impossible. Only You can make it
possible. Amen.

"Harriet," Montgomery called. He motioned
for her to go into the wheelhouse. Beth
continued working.

"What's the meeting about?" she asked
Walter.

"They're probably talking about the attack,"
he said. "They need to know the layout of
Heyward's plantation and the causeway."

"What's a causeway?" Beth asked.

The *Adams* rounded a curve in the
Combahee River. Walter pointed to a long land
bridge.

The causeway was narrow, the width of a

country lane. There were no trees, nothing to hide behind. The Confederate soldiers and plantation overseers would see anyone coming.

The Second South Carolina Volunteers will need to cross the land bridge, Beth thought. *They'll be in great danger.*

The *Adams* docked near the end of the causeway. Soldiers worked to lay planks of wood between the ship and the land.

The colonel and Harriet came out of the wheelhouse.

Montgomery shouted orders. About sixty Volunteers headed to the causeway.

Walter said, "I get to go ashore with this group of Volunteers." Walter waved and picked up his drum. He hurried after the soldiers.

Beth prayed for the Volunteers to be safe.

They started to march across the causeway, two men abreast. Walter was at the end, beating his drum.

The crack of a rifle shot filled the air.

Beth scanned the plantation to see where it had come from. She saw a white man with a rifle in the rice field.

None of the soldiers seemed to have been hit. The Volunteers kept marching to the beat of Walter's drum. They marched straight into enemy territory.

"Gunner, prepare to fire at that rifleman," shouted Montgomery.

The artillery regiment sprang to life.

The gunner squatted behind the cannon. He adjusted the height of the barrel.

"Load," shouted the gunner.

One soldier opened the ammunition box. Another carried the cone-shaped shell. He placed the shell in the mouth of the cannon.

The next man pushed the shell down the barrel with a rod.

"Ready," shouted the gunner.

One man fiddled with something on top of the cannon.

"Fire," shouted the gunner.

Another soldier pulled a string.

BOOM!

The cannon shot sailed overhead and landed in the rice field.

The enemy dropped his rifle and ran.

"Yay!" Beth cheered. The troops also cheered.

The first of the Volunteers stepped off the causeway. The rest soon followed. They fanned out into a rice field.

Harriet asked the colonel, "Is it time to blow the whistle?"

Montgomery nodded and shouted, "Call the slaves to freedom!"

The Raid

Boom!

Patrick's heart sank. The explosion came from the river. He didn't know if the cannon fire was from the Union ships. It could be from the Confederate artillery. Either way, it wasn't good.

Boom!

The slaves in the field stopped their work. They stood and shouted to one another.

Children ran to women and were comforted with hugs.

Patrick knew what he had to do. He couldn't stop the messenger. And he couldn't warn Montgomery about the Confederate troops.

But he could tell the slaves to flee to the ships.

A shrill whistle filled the air.

Patrick urged his horse into the rice fields. He reached a young woman with a small child in a sling that stretched across her shoulders.

"Run to the river," Patrick told her. "Union ships are on the Combahee. They'll take you to freedom."

She shook her head. It seemed she didn't understand.

Patrick wished Walter were there to speak her language.

"Freedom," Patrick shouted. He pointed toward the river. "Run!"

A man on horseback rode toward them through the fields. He had a whip in his hand.

Crack!

"To the woods," the man on horseback shouted at the slaves.

Some of the field workers started to follow him.

The slave woman's face grimaced in fear. She lifted the sling with the child off her shoulders. She thrust the child at Patrick.

"Freedom," she said with an odd accent.

Patrick took the sling and the child with tight, black curls. He quickly looped the sling over his shoulder.

"Go!" the woman said. Her voice was husky. There were tears in her eyes.

Patrick snapped the reins.

The child in his arms shrieked in terror.

The horse bolted toward the river.

● ● ●

Beth saw the slaves at the Heyward plantation stream toward the river. Old men with knobby knees and women with gray hair. Young children with knapsacks on their backs. Barrel-chested men. Teens. Women with babies on their shoulders and in their arms.

Most of them carried rice pots, chickens in cages, or sacks of food. One woman carried two young pigs, a black one and a white one.

The slaves hurried along the causeway or toward the river. Those at the river's edge seemed confused. They didn't move toward the empty rowboats.

"Why aren't they filling the boats?" Beth asked.

"They're scared. Slave owners won't let slaves learn to swim," Harriet said. "That makes it harder for them to escape."

Colonel Montgomery shouted at Harriet, "Do something with *your* people! Tell them to get to the boats."

Harriet frowned. "I'm black and a former slave," she said. "But I'm from Maryland. I don't speak Gullah. These aren't *my* people."

Beth said, "But God made them all. So they are *our* people."

Harriet beamed at Beth.

"Do something," the colonel shouted. "Or they'll lose their chance at freedom!"

Harriet climbed down the rope ladder to the remaining rowboat.

Beth followed her into the boat. It could easily carry six more people.

Harriet picked up a set of oars. So did Beth. They rowed toward the beach.

The slaves watched them. They murmured to one another when Harriet got out of the rowboat.

Harriet slowly waded into the water. The fabric of her dress billowed out at first. Then it soaked up water and clung to her legs. She started to sing in a calm, sweet voice: "Come from the east. Come from the west. Come along, come along."

A teen girl with a white head wrap moved away from the group. She waded toward the rowboat.

Harriet took the girl by the crook of the arm. Together they waded to the side of the rowboat.

Beth reached toward the girl. The slave clasped Beth's hand in a fierce grip. Beth pulled and helped her climb aboard the rowboat.

Harriet kept singing and motioning with her arms.

The others seemed to understand. They stepped into the water.

Harriet directed six more to the rowboat.

Beth pulled them in.

Then four more.

The boat sank lower in the water. It was overcrowded. Beth lifted the oars. A man sitting on the back bench watched her carefully. He put his hands on the oars near him.

Together, they rowed the boat to the side of the *Adams*.

Beth breathed a sigh of relief when the last person left the rowboat. She wrinkled her nose. She smelled smoke.

Beth took the oars and rowed back toward the river's edge. She glanced across the water toward the plantation. Union soldiers had set some of the buildings on fire.

Cows, pigs, goats, and one white sheep hurried along the causeway. The slaves behind them were running.

Then Beth heard rifle fire.

Heyward Plantation

Bang!

Patrick pulled on the reins to stop his horse. He took out the pocket watch and the captain's map. He glanced at the picture. The officer on the horse looked proud. The watch had Colonel William C. Heyward written on it.

The child pressed her face into his chest. He could feel her hot tears seeping into his shirt.

A breeze pushed the smoke away from him and the girl. He patted her tight, black curls.

He said, "It'll be okay. Miss Harriet will help you."

Patrick unfolded the map and studied it. He thought he was on the edge of the Heyward plantation.

He put the watch and map back in his pocket. Then he nudged the horse with his knees. They headed toward the Heyward plantation.

Bang. Bang. Bang.

Patrick heard the beat of a drum between shots.

Is that Walter's drum? he wondered.

He came to a dirt road leading to a large white house. Large oak trees grew on either side of the path. Their thick branches reached across the road to form a roof.

Patrick followed the road and reached the house.

House slaves were leaving. Their arms were full of kitchen pots and baskets of food.

Six or seven Volunteers were also leaving with supplies from the house. One carried a long sword.

That soldier grinned at Patrick. "We've got Master Heyward's sword!" he said. "He'll throw a fit when he finds out!"

The soldier squinted at Patrick. "Weren't you thrown off the *Adams*?" he asked.

"Yes," Patrick said. "But then I was assigned to the *Weed*. I need to get a message to Colonel Montgomery. The Confederate base has been warned about this raid. Rebel soldiers will be here soon."

The soldier said, "I'll tell my captain first. Then I'll tell Colonel Montgomery." He ran toward the river, the sword held above his head.

A house slave carrying a large basket moved away from the house.

Patrick called to her.

"Yes, sir," she said, approaching him. Her dress was nicer than that of the field workers. She had a neat white fabric cap on her head. She also wore an apron.

Patrick shifted the child so the woman could see her. "Will you take her to the ship?" he asked.

The woman nodded. She put down the basket and reached for the toddler. Patrick untied the sling and handed the girl to the woman. Then he dismounted and set the horse free.

The animal darted into the trees.

Patrick told the woman, "The little girl's mother is a slave on a distant field. An overseer stopped her from coming to the river. This girl has no family now."

"I'll see that she has a home," the woman said. She settled the girl inside the basket. "Grab one handle. I'll take the other. We'll get her to the river together."

Patrick and the woman carried the basket a few dozen feet. Suddenly a bare-chested slave came alongside them. He was three times the size of Patrick.

The man had dozens of raised scars on his back. Patrick had to stop himself from wincing when he saw them. They looked like welts from a whip.

The man said something to the woman in a language Patrick didn't understand. Then the woman said to Patrick, "He'll take the basket and the girl to the ship."

The man hoisted the basket in his

arms. He took off running toward the causeway.

The woman turned back to the house. "I'll get some more things from the cupboards," she said. "The Union soldiers will burn the house next."

"Wait," Patrick said. "Do you know a boy named Kitch?"

A sad look crossed the woman's face. "Everyone at the manor house knows the boy from Kentucky," she said. "He spoke proper English, so the master used him as a house servant."

Patrick's heart filled with hope. "Is he inside the house?" Patrick asked.

The woman shook her head. "Look down near the slave houses by the river," she said. "He's been here only two years. But he's tried to run away six times. The master's men shackled him."

● ● ●

Hours passed. Beth helped row one of the boats. Some of the time she stood in the water to help slaves into boats. Harriet and another Volunteer used a second rowboat.

About two hundred slaves had already boarded the *Adams* by the causeway ramp.

The overseers had fled the fields. They were most likely hiding in the nearby forest from Union soldiers.

Beth was sopping wet. Her wrists ached from helping so many into the rowboat.

A little girl in a large basket had just been put on Beth's rowboat.

Smoke from the fires stung Beth's eyes. She was tired.

But Harriet wasn't slowing down. She helped more and more field hands into her

rowboat. She motioned for others to walk
along the causeway.

The slaves broke out in song from time to time.
Some of the tunes sounded familiar to Beth. But
she didn't understand the Gullah words.

Somehow all the slaves knew how to say,
"Thank you" and "Bless you." Many said it
with smiles.

"Would you look at that!" Harriet said. She
pointed.

A Union soldier carrying a sword above his
head was running toward them. The slaves
let him through. He waded into the river up to
his waist.

"Colonel Montgomery!" the soldier shouted.
"The Rebels are coming!"

The colonel appeared at the edge of the
ship. He leaned over the side and shouted,
"Did you see them?"

"No!" the soldier said. "The boy you ordered

off the *Adams* is back! He brings an important
message."

Patrick! Beth thought. *He's okay.*

"Blast it," the colonel shouted. "A battle is
no place for children!" He slammed a fist on
the railing.

"The boy has news," the soldier said. "He
says a Confederate messenger warned the
Rebel soldiers about the raid."

The colonel shouted to Harriet, "Get the
rowboats to the ship. We're pulling out before
the enemy comes."

"All right," Harriet shouted back. "We want
no bloodshed today."

"Retreat," Montgomery shouted.

One of the soldiers on deck blew a horn. He
made a series of short notes.

Beth's throat tightened. She looked at the
shore. About fifty slaves waited. There wasn't
time to rescue them all.

Kitch

Patrick ran past the manor house toward the stables.

There were dozens of stalls. Union soldiers were releasing the horses.

Patrick got a whiff of kerosene. One soldier was pouring it from a can. He splashed the liquid on the walls and bags of feed. The stable would burst into flames once a fire was lit.

One Volunteer was leading a large, beautiful horse out of the last stall. The horse had a saddle on its back. It looked familiar.

Patrick took out the pocket watch. He compared the picture of the horse to the live one. Both horses had the same splotch of cream hair on their necks. The saddles were identical. But the live horse had a blue wool blanket under the saddle. The blanket had a gold star on it.

He remembered the message. *Follow the star.*

"Excuse me," Patrick said. "May I look at that saddle?"

The soldier cocked his head. "You may," he said. "But be quick. This stable is going up in flames soon. And the bugle call to retreat was just sounded."

Patrick searched on and around the saddle.

He didn't know what he was looking for. His hand felt a seam in the leather. He had found a pocket. Inside the pocket was a large key.

Patrick grabbed the key. "Thanks," he said to the Volunteer.

The soldier led the horse toward the river.

Patrick also headed toward the river. He saw a row of small houses close to the water. Each one had a stone chimney and a narrow front door.

At the end of the houses was a large post. A boy was shackled to the post. He had chains around his ankles and wrists. He was wearing only a pair of torn shorts.

Kitch!

Kitch was slumped against the pole and said nothing. It seemed as if he was too tired to care about freedom. But he wasn't alone. A woman and an older teen were trying to free

him. The young man was trying to break the chains with a hoe.

Clang. He swung the hoe again. *Clang.* But the chains held together.

The woman pushed on the post. But the wooden pole didn't budge.

"Hey," Patrick said. "I've got a key!" He hoped it would fit the lock.

The woman said, "Bless you."

Patrick's hands shook as he poked the key into the lock. He turned the key. *Click.*

The teen slave grabbed the lock and pulled it off.

Kitch's hands were free!

The woman started to weep. "Praise the Lord," she said.

Patrick looked back. Three of the barns were already burning. Smoke rose from the flames and licked the sky. The Volunteers were running along the causeway toward the *Adams.*

Patrick knelt and unlocked the shackles around Kitch's ankles.

Kitch was free!

The slave woman and teen came alongside Kitch. Each supported him at the shoulders.

They all moved toward the river's edge, step by step.

Patrick saw the line of slaves waiting on the causeway to board. Kitch was too slow to get there in time.

The bugle sounded again.

Are we too late? Patrick wondered.

The Last Rowboat

Beth was standing in the water near the shore.

Harriet was taking a rowboat full of freed slaves to the *Adams*.

The *Adams* paddlewheel started to turn. Smoke poured from its smokestack. The ship was getting ready to leave the plantation.

Walter rowed an empty boat toward Beth.

"Get in," Walter shouted to her.

Beth waded toward the rowboat. She reached to grab its side. Walter grabbed her wrists and pulled her inside.

"I'm not leaving without Patrick," Beth said.

"Neither am I," Walter said. He pointed to the shore.

Beth looked toward the burning manor house. Patrick and three slaves emerged from the smoke. One of the slaves could barely walk. A woman and a teen held him up by the shoulders.

"I found Kitch," Patrick called, waving. "I found him!"

"Hurry!" Beth said. "The *Adams* is leaving!"

Suddenly half a dozen slaves waded into the water toward the rowboat.

Walter spoke in a loud voice. But Beth couldn't understand his words. The slaves did.

"What did you say?" Beth asked.

"I told them the *Adams* is leaving. There

won't be enough room for everyone," Walter said.

Beth climbed over the rowboat's side. She slipped into the water again. "Patrick and I will be fine," she said to Walter.

Beth waded toward Kitch and the slaves next to him.

"Hurry!" she said.

The three of them waded into the water.

Beth and Patrick helped Kitch and his friends into the boat.

Walter spoke in Gullah again. Five other slaves moved toward the rowboat.

Kitch gave Beth a weak smile. Beth thought his smile looked a lot like Sally's.

"Your sister Sally sent us," Beth said. "She's safe in Canada."

"That's more than I'd hoped for," Kitch said.

Patrick pushed the rowboat away from the shore.

Walter said, "Get a horse. You have time to ride and meet us at Fields Point!"

"Don't worry about us," Patrick called. "We'll get home another way."

Beth heard a faint noise. It was a low humming sound. She looked around. There was a slight glow on the shore. The Imagination Station fully appeared.

Beth hoped it wouldn't disappear again. "Time to go home," she said to Patrick.

"Goodbye, Walter," Patrick yelled. "Tell Harriet goodbye for us. Ask her to nurse Kitch back to health."

"Maybe she can take Kitch to Canada when the war's over," Beth said.

Walter nodded. He rowed the last boat toward the *Adams* and freedom.

Beth and Patrick hurried to the Imagination Station.

Eugene was sitting in the driver's seat. He was still a teen.

Eugene said, "I did the impossible. President Lincoln helped me cross my own broken timeline. That's how I found the exact coordinates I needed. Then Mr. Whittaker and I programmed them into the Imagination Station. Now all we have to do is return to Odyssey."

"Didn't I see you on the Combahee River?" Beth asked.

"Perhaps you did," Eugene said. "I was split into quite a few stories for just an instant."

Patrick hopped into the Imagination Station first. He sat in the passenger seat. Beth climbed into the rumble seat.

Eugene said, "I see you've completed your mission as well."

"We did," Beth said. She smiled.

"Then there is only one thing left to do,"

Eugene said. He quickly pressed the red button.

The Combahee River seemed to rise and cover them until everything went black.

● ● ●

Patrick opened his eyes. He was in the basement workshop at Whit's End. "It's hard to believe that trip was real," Patrick said to Eugene. "We've been gone so long."

Mr. Whittaker was the grandfatherly inventor of Whit's End. He came up to the Model T and tapped on the windshield.

Patrick smiled at him.

"Eugene!" Whit said. "You're not too old. And you're not too young."

"Undeniably," Eugene said, grinning. "Our calculations were finally correct. I am my proper age, in spite of the Imagination Station's time warp."

Eugene got out of the Model T. Whit gave him a hug.

"I knew it would work this time," Whit said.

Beth stepped out of the rumble seat.

Patrick opened the door and left the passenger seat.

The cousins each hugged Whit. Then they hugged Eugene.

Patrick was happy to be home.

"I miss President Lincoln and Harriet Tubman already," Beth said.

Patrick nodded in agreement.

Whit stroked his moustache. "Abraham Lincoln was a brave president," he said. "Eventually he gave his life for his country."

"What happened to Harriet Tubman?" Patrick asked.

Whit leaned against the Model T. "She helped freed slaves learn to fend for themselves," he said.

"Like Kitch and those from the Heyward plantation?" Beth asked.

Whit nodded. "She served others till the day she died at age ninety-one," he said.

Patrick said, "It's going to be hard to come up with an adventure to beat this one."

Whit smiled.

Patrick saw his eyes twinkle.

"We'll see about that," Whit said.

Find out about the next adventure—*Poison at the Pump*—at ImaginationStation.com.

Secret Word Puzzle

Count the number of letters in each bold word. Find the column with the same number of boxes. Fill in the word. The first one has been done for you. The secret word is in the gray boxes.

Harriet Tubman   **Alligator**

Fields Point   **Tar** Bluff

John **Adams**   **Imagination** Station

Free   **Heyward** Plantation

Second South Carolina **Volunteers**

Go to TheImaginationStation.com.
Find the cover of this book.

Click on "Secret Word."

Type in the answer,

and you'll receive a prize.

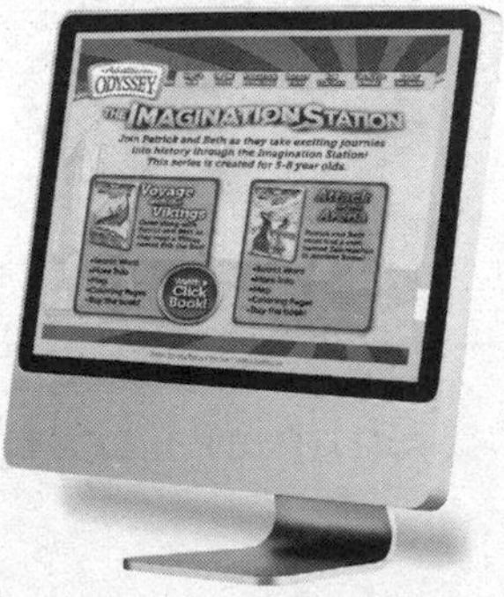

Authors and Illustrator

Author **Marianne Hering** has been making

reading fun since she joined the staff of Focus on the Family *Clubhouse* and *Clubhouse Jr.* magazines in 1987. Visit MarianneHering. com for more info about Harriet Tubman and other Imagination Station adventures.

Author **Sheila Seifert** is an editor, teacher,

and author or coauthor of several books for kids, including *Bible Kidventures: Stories of Danger and Courage*, which lets kids choose the direction of the story. Visit SimpleLiterature.com to learn more.

Born in Brazil, illustrator **Sergio Cariello** attended the Word of Life Bible Institute and  the Joe Kubert School of Cartoon and Graphic Art. He's worked as an art teacher and illustrator for many publishers, including Marvel, DC Comics, Disney, David C Cook, Crossgen, and Zondervan. He's also illustrated many books for Focus on the Family, including the Imagination Station series.